# Here in Space

## Written and Illustrated
## by David Milgrim

BridgeWater Books

*This book is dedicated
to everyone who wonders.*

**Library of Congress Cataloging-in-Publication Data**

Milgrim, David.
Here in space / written and illustrated by David Milgrim.
p.   cm.
Summary: An imaginative young "space explorer" describes
the many fascinating features of his home on the planet Earth.
ISBN 0-8167-4393-2
[1. Earth—Fiction. 2. Stories in rhyme.] I. Title.
PZ8.3.M5776He   1997
[E]—dc21                    97-11373

I live in space. I have lived here since birth,

On a big ball of rock that is called planet Earth!

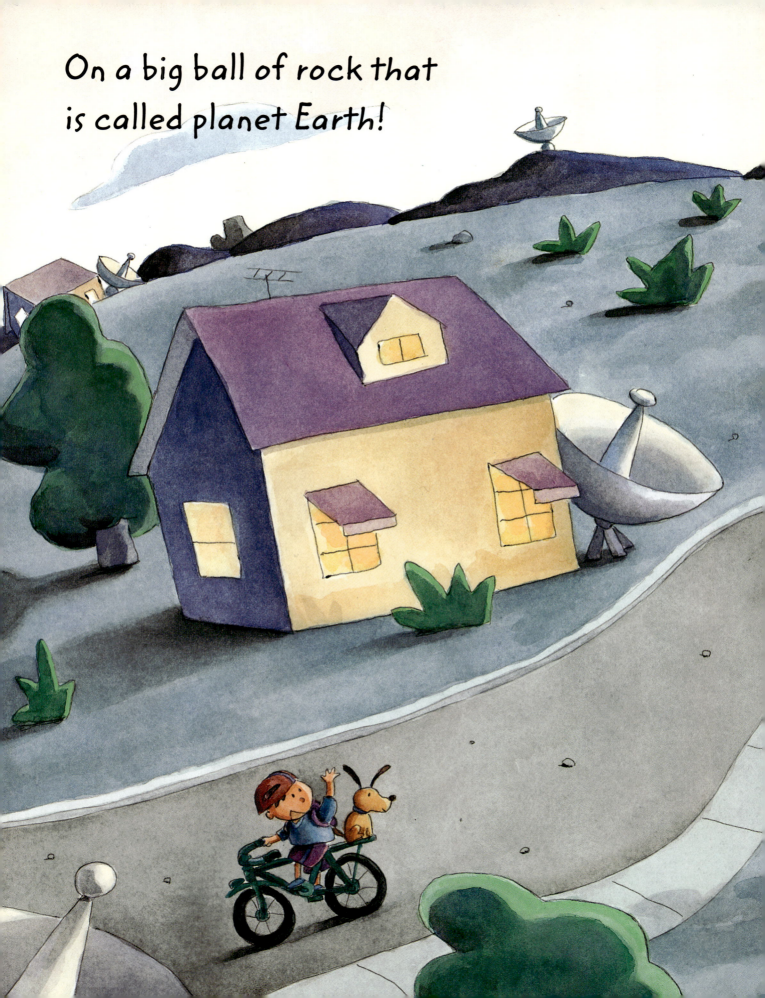

Since I live on the earth, I am living in space.

And space is a strange and mysterious place.

Out here in space there's a lot to explore.

There's fire that flames from
the earth's inner core.

There are oceans so cold that they freeze into land

And many strange creatures I don't understand.

In space there are powerful, thundering waves

And dark, eerie silences
deep in the caves.

There are man-made machines that can think on their own

And questions whose answers can never be known.

The earth is a wild,
exciting frontier.

And I am a rambling
space pioneer.

And here on the earth,
in this magical place,

I am always at home
in the wonder of space.